Digger Dan

Digger Dan

by
Patricia Lynn

Illustrations by
Si Frankel

Merrigold Press
Racine, Wisconsin

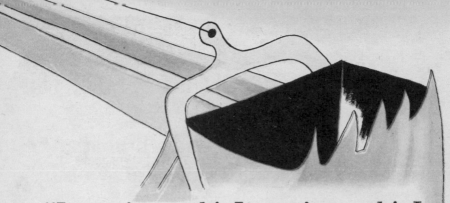

"I won't work! I won't work! I won't work today!" hissed Digger Dan.

"You never want to work first thing in the morning," said Stan the Steam Shovel Man. "But there's a job to be done. A school must be built on this very spot. We must dig out a basement. We must dig a whole lot!"

"Aha!" buzzed the big digger, "a school for boys and girls!" The more he thought about that school, the more he felt like working.

"I'll dig a deep, wide hole in the earth. I'll dig for all I'm worth!" he puffed.

And down went his dipper—open
wide. Gulp . . . then it closed, full
of earth inside.

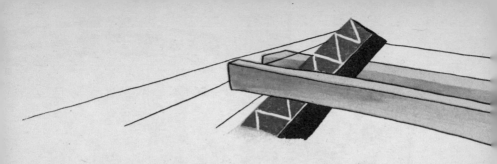

"Ready?" rattled Digger Dan to Big Dump Truck nearby.

"Ready!" tootled Big Dump Truck right back.

"Give me room," roared Dan to Stan the Steam Shovel Man.

"I need room
  To swing my boom!"

Push and pull, push and pull— soon Big Dump Truck was full.

"There you are. Take it far," Dan rumbled to the truck.

Then, for the first time, the big digger saw the children who waved to him as he worked.

"The steam shovel is big and strong!" they said.

Digger Dan waved back to all the children with his boom and bucket. Oh, but he was proud!

Day by day the basement hole grew and grew. One day it was all ready for the men to come and pour the concrete for the basement.

"My work is done," sang Dan. "Now I can play! Hurrah!"

But just at that moment who should come along but Farmer Turnipseed.

"Hi-ho!" said Stan the Steam Shovel Man.

"Good day," said the farmer, "and how do you do! I have a big job for your digger to do."

And the next morning there was Digger Dan crawling along out at the farm.

"I won't work! I won't work! I won't work today!" he clanked.

"Oh-ho!" shouted Stan the Steam Shovel Man. "But your job is to grade this land so the farmer can plant a vegetable garden."

"Aha!" thought the big digger. "The farmer wants to plant carrots and lettuce and corn for boys and girls to eat. Aha!"

The more Dan thought about those vegetables, the more he felt like working.

"I'll grade, and level, and smooth this earth. I'll dig and dig for all I'm worth!" clattered Dan, with a *rackety, rackety.*

"Dig and dump!" Stan shouted.
"Dig and dump,
   Take out every lump and bump!"

"Just watch me!" hummed Dan.
Down went his dipper ... open wide.
Gulp ... then it closed, full of rocks
inside.

"Digger Dan is clever!" said the children. "Digger Dan is smart!"

There was no stopping Dan after that!

Dig . . . Dump.

Clatter . . . Crash.

Down . . . Scoop

Swish . . . Swoop

Whirr . . . Chirr.

Pop . . . Pop . . . Pop!

Soon the land was ready for Farmer Turnipseed to plant his vegetables.

"My work is done," sang Dan. "Now I can play. Hurrah!"

But just at that moment who should come along but a small man with a big black mustache.

"Good day!" said the man to Stan. "Tomorrow please bring your digger to Fourth and Main—shine or rain!"

And the next morning there was Digger Dan crawling along at Fourth and Main, looking like a little house on wheels, yellow and fat, and wearing a smokestack for a hat.

"Away, away, away we roll,
   Off to dig another hole!" sang
Stan.

"But I won't work! I won't work!
I won't work today!" hissed Dan.
"A digger needs rest."

"We cannot rest," said Stan, "but how would you like to dig a basement for an apartment house—a place for boys and girls to live?"

"An apartment house!" buzzed Dan. "With a thousand windows to twinkle in the sunlight, and a roof garden where the children can play **all** day!"

The more Dan thought about that apartment house, the more he felt like working.

"Dump and dig," shouted Stan,
pushing his long levers every which
way.

"Dump and dig,
Make a hole that's plenty big!"

"Look," said the children who had come to watch. "That steam shovel knows just how to bite."

"Chug, puff, hiss,
    I like to do this!"
Dan hummed.

Then one day there were boys and girls going into the school Dan had helped to build.

There were children eating fresh
vegetables that grew on the farm
land he had graded.

There were children going up in the elevator of the apartment house Dan had helped to build.

Dan saw them all as he rolled away to dig a roadbed for a railroad.

Some day those children would go riding on a big streamliner, along shiny new rails.

Down . . . scoop! Swish . . . Swoop! went Digger Dan's dipper. Putter-put! Open and shut!

"I like to work," he said. "It seems like PLAY!"